DIARY
OF A
MINECRAFT
ZOMBIE

Book 13

by Zack Zombie

Friday –
September 13th

"**H**ey, Steve!"

"Wassup, Zombie?"

"Nuthin' Wassup with you?"

"Just punching a tree," Steve said. "Hey, what day is it today?"

"I think it's Friday," I said.

"Friday the what?" Steve asked.

"It's Friday the 13th. Why?"

"FRIDAY THE 13th?!!!! No way!"

I could tell from Steve's face turning a really bright shade of white that something really bad was going to happen.

It's not every day you can scare the bravest guy in Minecraft.

"Dude, you look really pale. What's up?"

"Well, remember I told you about that bully who used to bother me a few years ago?"

"Yeah, I think I remember him. The guy with the funny name. . .Harry something, right?"

"Harry O'Brien," Steve said with a really scared look on his face.

"Hey, didn't you tell me you stood up to him and he ran away or something?"

"Yeah, he ran away, and no one ever saw him after that," Steve said.

"Then why are you so scared? I thought he was gone for good."

"He's gone, yeah. But not for good." Suddenly, Steve had a look on his face like something really bad was going to happen.

"Whaddya mean?"

"Well, after I stood up to him, then all of the other villager kids stood up to him too. He was so embarrassed and after that, he just ran away."

"Serves him right. . ."

"Yeah, well, what no one knew was that he ran away and ended up in the Abandoned Cave."

Steve said it with his scary voice. Kinda like when you get a really big lump of snot in your throat and you can't get it out. . .but not as tasty.

"The what?" Now I was starting to get creeped out.

"The Abandoned Cave. You never heard of it? It's supposed to be haunted with the spirit of the Wicked Witch of the Well."

"The wicked what of the who?!!!"

"You know, the Wicked Witch of the Well," Steve said, like I knew he was talking about.

"Who's that?" I asked, not really wanting to know the answer.

"You never heard of the Wicked Witch of the Well?"

"Uh, no. . .Gulp."

"Well, she's a Witch. . .and she, um. . .lives in a well. . .and she's, uh, wicked. . .really, you never heard of the Wicked Witch of the Well?"

"No. . .who is she?"

"Actually, I really don't know," Steve said. "All I know is that she's supposed to haunt the Abandoned Cave. And she's supposed to grant you a wish if you're desperate enough to sell her your soul."

Now I was really getting scared.

"So, what does that have to do with you?"

"Well, Harry found the Witch in the Abandoned Cave and he made a deal with her to get revenge on me."

"What the what?!!

"Yeah, crazy, right?" Steve said.

"But, how did you know he did all that?"

"Well, he visits me every Friday the 13th and reminds me of our big fight."

"What fight?"

"Well, the Witch granted him one wish, and his wish was to fight me to the death on the next October, Friday the 13th."

"Seriously?!!"

"Yeah. The good thing is there hasn't been a Friday the 13th in October in a couple years. . ."

"Whew, that's close," I said.

"Until this year. . ."

"What?!!!"

"Yeah, this is the only year when Friday the 13th lands in September and October," Steve said with a scared look on his face. "So next month, I need to fight Harry to the death."

"What are you going to do?"

"I've gotta train, that's what I'm going to do." Then Steve jumped up and started punching a tree.

"Uh. . .Steve. . .you think you can beat him?"

"I don't know. You see, the Witch also gave him special powers so he can beat me. She even gave him a new name."

"Really, what's his name now?"

"He calls himself Herobrine."

7

CLAPBOOM!

All of sudden, we heard a loud clap of thunder in the background.

"Herobrine?!!"

CLAPBOOM!

"Yeah, Herobrine."

CLAPBOOM!

"Hey, wait a minute. . .Herobrine."

CLAPBOOM!

"Herobrine."

CLAPBOOM!

"He, He, He, Ro, Brine, Brine, Brine. . ."

CLAP, CLAP, CLAP, BOOM, CL-CL-CL-CLAP!

"Man, this is fun!"

"That's not funny, Zombie. I gotta get ready."

"Sorry, man. Anything I can do?"

"Naw, I got this," Steve said, punching blocks out of his tree.

"All right man, I'll see ya."

Steve didn't say goodbye, but I didn't mind.

I mean, he had to prepare for his death match with this Herobrine character in a few weeks.

CLAPBOOM!

What the what? Hey, I was only thinking that!

Well, anyway. This guy, Hero. . .

CCCLLAA. . .

...Uh, I mean, the guy formerly known as Harry O'Brien sounds really tough. Especially with super powers.

I mean, Steve's tough and all but he doesn't have special powers.

The only super power he has is punching trees.

And eating loads of cake.

Wow...in a few weeks, I might lose the best friend I've ever had.

Man, I need to do something!

But what can I do?

...What can I do?

Friday, September 13th
Later that day. . .

After dinner, I decided to go see Steve.

I thought I would cheer him up with a couple of pieces of my mom's cake.

As I was about to make it to Steve's house, all of a sudden a ball of fire came out of nowhere and started hovering above Steve's house.

I saw Steve outside when, suddenly, somebody jumped out of the ball of fire. . .

It was another Steve!

Except this other Steve had glowing white eyes, and he was hovering a few feet above the ground.

"What do you want now, Harry!" Steve yelled at the other Steve.

"I'M NOT HARRY, I'M HEROBRINE!"

CLAPBOOM!

"Yeah, whatever. You're still Harry to me. Or, what did your mom used to call you? Oh, yeah, Stinky."

CLAPBOOM!

"WAIT, WHAT. . .THAT SHOULDN'T HAPPEN. IT SHOULD ONLY HAPPEN WHEN YOU. . ."

"Whaddup, Stinky?"

CLAPBOOM!

"HEY, STOP THAT. . .I MEAN IT! OR ELSE. . ."

"Or else what, Stinky?"

CLAPBOOM!

"URRRGGGHHH!!!!"

All of sudden, Steve's house burst into flames.

BOOOOM!!!

"SEE WHAT YOU MADE ME DO! URRGGHH! YOU JUST WAIT TILL FRIDAY THE 13TH, YOU GOT YOURS COMING!!!"

Then the other Steve jumped into his fireball and disappeared.

Then Steve ran to put his house fire out.

"Hey, Steve, you need a hand?"

"No worries, I got it." Steve pulled out a potion bottle with water in it.

Then he threw the potion bottle at the house and a big waterfall appeared over his house and put the fire out.

"Who was that?"

"That was Harry. I told you he comes every Friday the 13th to remind me of our fight."

"Dude, you gotta fight him? That guy could totally incinerate you!"

"Yeah, probably."

"Why don't you just say no?"

"Well, he said if I don't fight him, then he'll destroy everybody I care about. . .oh, yeah, and he'll probably destroy all life on Minecraft too."

"Seriously?!!!"

"Yeah, so, I need to get back to training!" Steve said, and he started punching trees again.

"Steve, I hate to break it to you but I don't think punching trees is going to help you against that guy."

"Yeah, maybe. But we got some really thick trees around here," Steve said as he continued punching his tree.

"Uh, I have some cake for you. . .my mom made it."

Steve just looked at me and smiled.

"You eat it. I've got training to do," Steve said as he continued to punch his tree.

"Oh, OK."

Wow, Steve wasn't in the mood for cake.

Now I know we're in big trouble.

Saturday

What the what?!!!!

I got ten Subscribers to my latest Me-Tube Video!

I'm the Man! I'm the Man!

Mmph! Mmph! Mmph! Mmph!

(That's me doing my happy dance, by the way. . .)

Yeah!

Superstah!

If you didn't know, I just started uploading some of my sweet gaming skills on Me-Tube.

Me-Tube is like Z-Tube, but for gamers. Kinda like G-Tube, but for cool kids. But nothing like Noob-Tube. . .Eeeww! No way!

I started uploading my videos 'cause I figured if I'm this awesome, I might as well let the world know about it.

Also, I was hoping to make a few bucks with it too.

That's because my allowance is so small, I can't even pay attention.

"Hey, Creepy! Check it out! I got ten new subscribers!"

"Really, let me see. . .Whoa, that is so cool."

"Yeah, I know, right?"

"Hey, how come you don't turn on the comments?" Creepy said. "Sometimes it's good to hear people's constructive criticism, you know."

"Uh, yeah, I guess so. . .Let me see. . .There! Comments on!"

Blink!

Blink!

"Wow, those comments are really streaming in. . ."

Blink! Blink! Blink!

"Yeah, you probably had a bunch of unread comments that just popped up. What do they say?"

"Let me see. . .Here's one. . .

"THIS GUY IS A REAL NOOB. . ."

"What the what?!!!"

"Here's another one. . .

"THIS GUY PLAYS LIKE HE'S GOT SQUARE HANDS OR SOMETHING. . ."

"Huh!"

"Let me see that Zombie," Creepy said. "Maybe you're not reading it right. . .Uh, here's a good one. . ."

"THIS GUY IS PLAYING REALLY GOOD. . .FOR A NOOB. . .HE'S PROBABLY USING A HACK."

"Hey! If they didn't like it, why do I have so many subscribers?"

"Oooooh. . .SSSSSSSS. . .I think this next comment explains why. . ."

"ME AND MY FRIENDS SUBSCRIBED TO THIS NOOB'S CHANNEL BECAUSE WE FIGURED HE PROBABLY DIDN'T HAVE ANY FRIENDS."

"What the what?!!!"

"Sorry, Zombie. But forget about it, man. Those are just a bunch of haters who don't have anything better to do. They don't know what they're talking about."

Blink!

"YOUR ME-TUBE ACCOUNT HAS BEEN SUSPENDED BECAUSE OF YOUR LOW SKILL STATUS. PLEASE WORK ON YOUR SKILLS BEFORE YOUR ACCOUNT CAN BE REACTIVATED, NOOB."

"Aw, man!"

"Hey, Zombie, don't worry. Look, it says you can still upload your videos here. . ."

"PLEASE FEEL FREE TO UPLOAD YOUR VIDEOS ON NOOB-TUBE. . .NOOB."

"What the wha. . .?!!"

All I could do was sit there and stare at my computer screen wondering why this could be happening to me.

I mean, if the kids on Me-Tube don't like me, then who even does?

Man, I'm such a Noob.

I think I'm going to change my name. . .

Sunday

I went to go see Steve again to see how he was holding up.

I mean, it's not every day that a demon makes a threat to wipe your existence off the face of Minecraft.

But I just couldn't get my mind off those comments those kids said on Me-Tube.

Like, am I really a Noob?

I thought I had some sweet skills. I mean, I beat my little brother about ten times in a row.

And I've beat all my friends, even though they're all Noobs.

And I even beat one of the top Minecraft players once by accident.

23

Hmm. . . Maybe it's time I played somebody more advanced.

Somebody like. . .Yeah!

Darius Flenderman. . .The Enderman.

Darius is like the gaming champ for miles around.

Man, if I beat him, then everybody will know I'm not a Noob.

As I was crossing the street to go to Steve's house, I saw a group of Enderman kids hanging out moving stuff.

Man, I still can't understand why they do that.

I looked at one of them and just nodded to say, "Wassup."

"Whatya' staring at. . .Noob?"

"Uh, nothing. Sorry."

24

Man, I forgot. Enderman don't like to be stared at.

So, I made it to Steve's house and Steve was still out punching trees.

"Sup, Steve, whatcha doing?"

"I'm punching this tree."

"Uh...OK...so how are you doing with all the Friday the 13th Demon death match stuff?"

"I'm getting ready! I've gotta keep training!" Steve said as he kept punching the tree.

"Hey, isn't that the same tree you were punching a few days ago? Aren't you going to try other stuff?

"Like what?"

"Well, why don't you try the Super-Death-Lock Choke Hold or the Paralyzing Double

Slam Back Breaker move. . .You know, like they do on The Ultimate Zombie Fighters or on ZFC's Body Slammers 3000."

"I could do that stuff. But, like my old sensei used to say. . . 'Fear not the man who has punched ten thousand trees, but fear the man who has punched the same tree ten thousand times."

"Whoa. . . sounds like that guy really doesn't like trees."

Steve just looked at me.

"Anyway, you need any help?" I asked.

"Yeah, I need something to practice my punch on. You up for it?"

"Sure."

Now, I didn't really think Steve would punch me. Or if he did, I didn't think he would punch me that hard. . .You know, because

I was his friend, right? And, you know,
punching trees is really weird and stuff. . .

BOOM!

POP!

All of a sudden, I felt a really strong draft in
my nether regions.

I didn't think much of it until I saw Steve
chasing my bony legs around a tree.

Then I heard something that sounded like a
balloon deflating.

PSSSSSSSSSS.

When I finally realized what happened, Steve
walked over to me and I looked up at his
face. Then he burst out laughing.

"Herr, thass nat furry, man. Herp me upf!"

Steve tried to help me up, but without my
bones, he couldn't hold me up for long. So,

27

he just took me and just hung me on a tree branch like an old sheet.

Then he looked me over with a really strange smile on his face.

Next thing I know, Steve's putting my skin on like an old coat.

"Hey, look at me!" Steve said. "I gotta new Minecraft skin!"

"Her, come urn! Sterp that!"

Steve just kept on, "UURRGGHH! I'm a Zombie, and I eat boogers. . .ha, ha!"

But after he had his laughs, Steve just hung me back on the tree.

"Hey, I'll go get your legs," Steve said. "And the way your arms shot off like that, I think they're probably at my village by now."

"Wherd about my skurl?"

"Your skull. . . Uh, it's gotta be around here somewhere. Don't worry, I'll find it."

A few hours later, Steve came back with my arms, legs, and my spine. . .Yeah, I forgot I had one of those too.

"Oh, man. . .what happened to you? You look like a green balloon with legs."

"Uh. . .Old Man Jenkins found me and he patched me up," I said. "He said the same thing happened to him when he worked at the TNT factory."

"Wow, that's a lot of duct tape." Steve said as he burst out laughing again. "And what did he fill you up with helium?"

"Hey, that's not funny!" I said in a squeaky voice.

PSSSSSSSSSS!!!!

"See, now I sprung a leak. Help me patch it up."

"You sure you want your arms and legs back? You could just float home, you know."

That was actually a good idea. I was feeling a little lightheaded.

So, Steve tied a rope to me and he carried me home like a big green balloon.

When I got home, I put my arms and legs back but I had a hard time keeping my head up without a skull.

What could I use? I thought.

The only thing I could find was a big couch cushion.

Now my head looks like a big jigsaw puzzle.

Wow, now I look like a real Noob.

Monday

Today at lunchtime, all the kids were talking about our upcoming Mob Middle School Dance Party.

They decided to make it a costume party to make up for the fact that the school won't allow us to have a Halloween party anymore.

I think people are too scared of another Zombie Apocalypse.

"Hey, what are you coming as?" Creepy asked me.

"I think I'm going to come as a Noob," I said.

"Really? What does a Noob look like?"

"You're looking at him," I said.

"Zombie, you're not still mad about getting banned from Me-Tube, are you?"

"Whoa, you got banned from Me-Tube?!!!" Skelly asked. "I thought that only happens to Noobs. Like, really, really bad Noobs."

That did not make me feel any better.

"But you can always sign up for Noob-Tube. I hear they'll take anybody," Skelly said.

"Dude, not helping," Creepy said.

"Cheer up, Zombie," Skelly said. "The Dance Party is coming up in a few weeks, and by then you'll totally forget about being a Noob."

"Dude, still not helping."

Then Slimey came by and sat down at our table.

"Hey, who are you guys taking to the dance party? I heard this year we can bring dates."

"Are you serious?!!!!" we all asked in surprise. . .or horror. Couldn't tell.

"Yeah, it's one of the cool benefits of being in eighth grade," he said with a smug look. "We ain't kids no more."

"Whoa. . ." all of us said as we looked to the sky.

"Wow, you guys are real losers," Rachel said.

Rachel Patella. She was like the meanest Wither skeleton girl that ever lived in all of Minecraft.

I try to ignore her, but she just resurfaces every year in one of my classes.

Not to mention that she's lived across the street from my house for as long as I can remember.

I try not to talk about her, either, because if I mention her name I'll probably get cursed or something.

Especially since her mom is a Witch.

It's probably the reason why she's so mean.

Or maybe it's because her dad is a Wither.

She's probably really mean because she has to deal with four parents instead of two.

Sheesh! No wonder she's got issues.

Now, the funny thing is that Skelly has had a crush on Rachel since second grade.

But she won't give him the time of day.

Poor guy. He just sat there looking at her with his mouth open.

Rachel just gave him a look that I think burned a hole in his head.

Either that or Skelly's been playing with the stapler again.

But, anyway, let me stop talking about Rachel before I get cursed.

What I'd rather think about is who I'm going to take to the Dance Party.

36

But, seriously, who's going to go out with a Noob like me?

You know, the girl I really want to take to the Halloween party is Carrie.

Carrie Flenderman. She's an Enderman, like her cousin Darius.

But she'll never go out with me.

She's in high school, and she's the cousin of my new mortal enemy, Darius.

Not to mention I'm a Noob.

Man, that's three strikes. No way she'll ever go out with me.

But, you know. . .if she did say yes, then we could just teleport to the Dance Party.

Or we could spend time talking about what it's like being on the girls' basketball team.

And if there was an awkward silence, we could just move stuff around to pass the time.

But, man, who am I kidding?

Carrie would never go out with me as long as I'm a Noob.

That's why I need to beat her brother, Darius, in a one on one PVP Minecraft Death Match in front of everybody.

Then everybody will know I'm not a Noob.

And Carrie will say yes and go to the Dance Party with me.

But how am I supposed to beat Darius?

He's like the number one player in twelve biomes.

I don't know, but I'd better think fast.

The Dance Party is only a few weeks away, and I don't want to go as myself. . .

The Noob.

Tuesday

A BABYSITTER?!!!! NO WAY!!!

"Don't give me any lip, young man," my mom said. "You know what happened the last time your father and I left you alone with Wesley."

"Lip?"

"Zombie, you know what I mean."

I guess my mom is still mad at me for blowing up the kitchen last time she and Dad went out.

Still, it could've been worse.

I mean, it's not like Wesley needed his baby teeth anyway.

DING, DONG!

"There she is now," my mom said. "Zombie, please go get the door while your father and I finish getting ready."

UUURRRGGHHH!!!

Just when I thought I was really progressing in my life, my mom has to go and send me back to Noobsville.

DING, DONG!

"All right already, I'm coming!"

Then I opened the door and I couldn't believe my eyes. . .

"Hi, Zack."

"Uhhhh. . .hi. . .Carrie. . .Uhhhh. . .what are you doing here?"

"Oh, I see you met Carrie," my mom said, coming down the stairs. "Carrie is Harold Flenderman's daughter. Harold works with your father at the Nuclear Waste Plant, and she volunteered to watch you and your brother Wesley tonight."

"Uhhhhhh. . ."

"Zombie, close your mouth; you're drooling again."

"Uhhhh. . ."

"Carrie, don't mind him. Zombie just hit puberty and he's going through changes, you know. Like, last month he started growing this mole on his. . ."

"MOM!!!!!"

"It's OK, Mrs. Zombie. I know Zack. He goes to my cousin Darius' middle school. You're one year behind me, right, Zack?"

"Uhhhh. . ."

"Well, we need to go now," my mom said. "Wesley is up in his room and as soon as Zombie stops drooling, he'll show you around the house. Right, Zombie?"

"Uhhhh. . ."

"OK, I'll leave you to it. Goodbye, Carrie. Goodbye, Zombie."

"Uhhhh. . ."

For some reason, I couldn't get my mouth to move. It's like my mouth was frozen and all I could do was just stand there and look like a Noob.

"Zack, do you want to show me around your house?"

"Uhhhh. . ."

"Oookay, I think I'll find my way around."

Carrie went upstairs to Wesley's room, and I just stood there like a Noob.

Eventually, I was able to move my body away from the door and swim through my puddle of drool, and make it to my room.

Man, I can't believe it! Carrie Flenderman is in my house!

I called Skelly on my cell phone.

RING.

"Sup, Zombie, whatcha doin?"

"Dude! You are not going to believe this! Carrie Flenderman is in my house. She's babysitting me and Wesley!"

"SSSSS. . .Ooooohhh, babysitting? Bro that's like a Noob death sentence. I hope your mom didn't start dropping the puberty stories. . ."

"Uh. . .yeah."

""SSSSS. . .Ooooohhh, well, we can still salvage this one. But you gotta be real cool. Like super cool. I mean like, Liquid Nitrogen cold."

"Cool, I can do that. What else."

"That's it man. Just act cool. . .and whatever you do, don't stare at her because. . ."

CLICK.

What the what?!!!

Oh, man, my battery died!

Man, this phone has got the battery life of a fat Creeper at a surprise party.

"OK. . . I need to be cool. . .C'mon, Zombie, be cool. . .Be coooooooooool."

Carrie and Wesley were playing downstairs in the living room.

As I started to come down with my coooooooool attitude, I saw Carrie and I froze again.

I just couldn't stop staring at how beautiful she was, just sitting there, playing with Wesley. . .

Then she saw me staring.

All of a sudden. . .

"AAAAAAAAAHHHHHHH!!!!!!!," Carrie yelled.

"What the wha. . .?!!!!!"

Next thing I know, she teleported and she was gone!

Oh, man, I was so scared, I peed myself.

"Again! Again! Again!" Wesley was crying out.

It didn't seem to bother Wesley. . .but I still couldn't move, I was so scared.

Man, I knew I shouldn't have stared at her.

She probably thinks I'm a stalker or something.

Oh, man, now she'll never go out with me now.

Man, I'm such a Noob.

And now, I'm all wet. . .

Wednesday

Well, my mom and dad were really mad when they got home and Carrie was gone.

They thought I scared her on purpose.

I guess they couldn't believe that someone as sweet and cute as Carrie could go all crazy and teleport away.

So, I'm grounded again.

But I still like Carrie, though. Even with all her drama.

She's just passionate, that's all.

But, man, after yesterday, I need to find a way to win her over.

50

But how's a middle school Zombie Noob like me going to win over the prettiest girl in high school?

Thursday

Today, Ms. Bones decided to take us on another school field trip.

Something about going to an abandoned mineshaft.

I used to like field trips when I was a kid.

But now that I'm in eighth grade, I figured I'm just too cool for field trips.

Yeah, field trips are for Noobs.

When we got there, we had to go through a big cave to get into the abandoned mineshaft.

All the other kids started acting all scared like if they we're still in seventh grade.

"Hey, did you hear?" Creepy asked.

"Hear what?"

"Some of the kids think this abandoned mineshaft is haunted," Creepy said.

"Haunted? Man, what Noobs. There's no such things as haunted mineshafts," I said.

"Really," Slimey chimed in, looking scared. "Because they say that this mineshaft has a big well in the middle and they say a Witch lives there."

"Wait. . .what? Did you say there's a well, and a Witch, and she lives in the well in the middle of the abandoned mineshaft?"

"Yeah, it supposed to be right at the end of this cave," Creepy said.

"Seriously?!!!"

Oh man, this must be the haunted cave that Steve was talking about. And, if that's true. . .

53

THE WICKED WITCH OF THE WELL LIVES HERE!

The closer we got to the well, the more creeped out the other kids were getting.

Not me, of course. . .

OK, yeah, I was getting creeped out too.

"I bet you she eats Zombie flesh," Zeke, the zombie, said.

"I bet you she eats old bones," Maxilla and Scapula, the skeleton sisters, said.

"I bet you she eats Endernuggets," Glendy, the Enderman, said.

"What are Endernuggets?" somebody asked.

"You know, Enderman chopped up and turned into bite-sized nuggets, Duh!" Glendy said.

Whoa!

"I bet you she eats gunpowder," Alastair, the Creeper, said.

Man, I wasn't sure if anything the kids were saying was true, but I was really scared.

At the end of the cave was the abandoned mineshaft with a giant well in the middle of it.

But by then, we were all so creeped out we totally forgot all about the field trip.

Ms. Bones was acting like she wasn't scared, but I heard her knees knocking a few times.

"This is the scene of the great trial of the Wanda Witch Hazel," Ms. Bones began to tell us. "Many years ago, there was a Witch that was accused of poisoning human villagers. She would use her poison on unsuspecting villagers that she would catch mining for diamonds during the wee hours of the night."

Whoa, Steve wasn't kidding, I thought.

"And she was finally caught because she not only poisoned villagers, she started poisoning Minecraft mobs as well!"

CLAPBOOM!

Whoa!

Was that thunder! I thought. *How are we able to hear it down here, anyway?*

"Ms. Bones," Creepy said, slowly raising his hand. . .or his foot. . .I can't tell anymore.

"Yes, Creepy?"

"Why did she poison Minecraft Mobs?"

"Well, legend has it that she somehow got a taste for Mob flesh and she became obsessed with it!"

CLAPBOOM!

"HUH!" All of us gasped.

Ms. Bones continued her lecture, "The Witch
was finally caught, and her punishment
was to live at the bottom of this well for all
eternity!"

CLAPBOOM!

All of us were so scared, we were frozen to
the spot.

All of sudden, a creepy girl with black hair
started walking out of the well!

"AAAAAAAHHHHHHH!!!!!!!"

"IT'S THE WICKED WITCH OF THE WELL!" somebody yelled.

All the kids started screaming and yelling and running back.

Not even Ms. Bones was expecting that. At least her head wasn't because it quickly shot off her neck like a missile.

Yeah. . .she tends to loser her head a lot in stressful situations.

Me and the guys ran out of there so fast, we didn't even notice that we went the wrong way.

And then we ended up in another cave that was a dead end!

"Oh man, oh man, oh man, oh man!" Slimey started saying.

"What are we going to do?" Skelly said.

"TSSSSSSSSSSS," was all Creepy had to say.

Suddenly, we saw a shadow of a creepy girl crawling close and closer to us.

59

"She's coming!" Skelly yelled.

Then the Witch walked into our cave and all we could do was crouch together in a corner in a little ball.

"WE'RE GONNA DIE! MOMMY, MOMMY, MOMMY, MOMMY, MOMMY!" I couldn't help myself.

That's it. . .it's over. . .Goodbye world. . .

Then we heard somebody bust out laughing.

"What the what?!!!!" we all said.

When we looked up, all we could see was Rachel Patella in a black wig and creepy Witch clothes.

"Do you like these?" Rachel asked in between her laughter. "They're my mom's for when she goes out on the town."

"SERIOUSLY?!!!"

"Wow, you guys are real lions," Rachel said sarcastically. "I'd hate to be caught with you guys in a fight."

Then, she strutted out the cave like she owned us for life.

Me and the guys just looked at each other.

And they we started smiling. . .and then laughing. . .then high fiving each other.

I think we were all just glad we were still alive.

CLANG!

"AAAAAAAAAHHHHH!!!!!"

Then we just ran out of there as fast as we could.

Sunday - A few days later. . .

I lost my diary. . .cough. . .I mean journal, in the abandoned mineshaft the other day.

But, I wasn't brave enough to go back and find it.

So I had to wait till today to get my allowance and get a new one.

I just hope no one finds my diary and reads it.

I would probably die of total embarrassment if somebody every got their hands on that thing.

But I probably shouldn't worry.

I don't think anybody is crazy enough to go back to that place.

I hope. . .

Monday

Today, they announced that Greendale Mob High School's ninth grade class was going to host our school Dance Party.

And guess who was going to be running the decoration committee?

That's right! My future girlfriend, Carrie Flenderman!

They asked for some eighth graders to volunteer, so you know I had to do it to get close to Carrie.

"I'll dazzle her with my decorating skills," I told Slimey.

"Dude, what decorating skills? The only colors you know how to match are turquoise and blue."

"You'll see, I'll be like Michelangelo."

"You mean the Ninja Turtle?"

"UUUURRGGGHHH. Forget it."

"Hey, there she is again," I said as I watched her holding her clipboard with her long arms. I just love how she. . .

"Dude, you're staring at her. . .You'd better stop or she'll think you're stalking her again."

I just couldn't help looking at Carrie as I watched her gracefully use her long legs to walk over the tables in the gym to show us where she wanted the decorations to go.

As I stared at her moving gracefully around the gym, I. . .

"AAAAAHHHH!!!!"

. . .Bumped into Rachel.

"Ewww, stalker," Rachel said as she looked down on me with her big black eye sockets.

I just tried to ignore her like I usually do and get another glance at Carrie, but by then Carrie left.

"Thanks a lot, Rachel."

"Dude, you really need to get a life," she said as she slithered away.

Tuesday

I got the weirdest email today.

It went something like this. . .

>> (scroll down)

>>

>>

>>Now make a wish!!!

>>

>>

>> No, really, go on and make one!!!

>>

>>

67

>> Oh, please, she'll never go out with you!!!

>>

>>

>>But, if you send this email to 5096 people in the next five seconds, your wish will totally come true!

Oh man, my finger hurts.

. . .And I totally lost count.

>> (scroll down some more)

>>

>>

>> But if you don't send it to exactly 5096 people, you will grow a mole that will grow and grow, and then it will turn into a mad

goat that will murder you and throw you off a high building into a pile of cow poo. And then a human will eat your brain and turn your entrails into a belt to hold up his pants for all eternity. It's true! Because, THIS letter isn't like all of those fake ones, THIS one is TRUE!! Really!!!

Aw, man, I'm doomed!

WAAAAAAHHHH!!!!!

Well, it's a good thing these things are fake.

Gulp!

I hope. . .

Wednesday

"**Z**ombie, your father and I need to go to a special PTA meeting tonight, and I called a babysitter to watch you and Wesley again."

"Sure, anything you say, Mom."

"Now, I don't want to hear any lip young. . .wha?"

I guess my mom wasn't ready for that. But this is my chance to make it up to Carrie for scaring her last time.

"It's no problem, Mother. I'll be on my best behavior," I said.

"LIONEL! QUICK! ZOMBIE IS DELIRIOUS. HE MUST'VE EATENT THOSE BERRIES FROM THE GARDEN AGAIN!"

"Mom, I'm all right. I just realized the error of my ways, and I am attempting to make up for all my past mistakes."

My mom just looked at me like she wasn't sure whether to rush me to the hospital or drop down on her knees and praise Mojang.

DING DONG!

"Well. . .there she is," my mom said. "Zombie, could you go downstairs and get the door while your father and I finish getting ready?"

"Absolutely, Mother, anything for you."

Yes! This is my chance to really impress Carrie.

C'mon, Zombie, you can do this. . .Remember, act real cool, like Liquid Nitrogen.

71

I just had to practice my cool voice a little before I opened the door.

"Hey, baby, wasssahappening?"

Nah! That won't work. Let me try that again.

"Hey, doll, we're not socks. But I think we'd make a great pair."

No, no, no. . .

"Hey, Darlin', are you an alien? Because you just abducted my heart?"

DING DONG!

"ZOMBIE! Please get the door!" my mom yelled.

Well, here it goes. . .

I opened the door and looked up so I could look into Carrie's beautiful purple eyes, when all of a sudden. . .

"No. . .No. . .NONONONONONONO. . .
NOOOOOOOOOOOOOOOOO!"

"Oh, hi, Rachel," my mom said as she and
Dad came down the stairs.

"Hi, Mr. and Mrs. Zombie," Rachel said.

"You know Zombie, right, Rachel? I don't
know why he's sitting in the corner rocking
back and forth like that. But you know,
he's going through puberty right now and
strange things are happening to his body. Like
yesterday, he started growing this mole. . ."

"MOM!"

"It's OK, Mrs. Zombie. Zombie and I go way
back. I'm used to his funny behavior," Rachel
said as she gave me a menacing look, like I
wouldn't make it past the night.

"I'm sorry to call you at the last minute,
but we had some problems with our last

babysitter," my mom said as she also gave me a menacing look.

"No problem, Mrs. Zombie. I've been wanting to catch up with Zombie for a long time."

Oh, man. I knew I was in trouble.

"How's your mom and dad?" my dad asked Rachel. "I miss spending time with them."

"They're fine, Mr. Zombie. They have fond memories of you and Mrs. Zombie too."

"Oh, great. Well, Wesley is upstairs in his room, and when Zombie gets up from the floor he'll show you around the house," my mom said. "Goodbye, Rachel. Goodbye, Zombie."

"NONONONONONO. . ."

Last thing I heard was the dungeon door creaking and closing shut as it closed for the last time, leaving me to rot for all of eternity.

"You're mine now, HAHAHAHAHAHAHA!"

I recognized that maniacal laugh from the days when my mom and dad used to let Rachel watch me when we were kids.

I still can't remember much from those days. But, it's probably better that way. It was probably so traumatizing that my young mind just blocked it out to protect me.

"All right, Noob. Where's the food? I'm hungry."

A few hours into my prison sentence and after Rachel ate most of the food in the fridge, it started to rain and thunder outside.

RUMBLE. . .CLAPBOOM!

75

Suddenly, all the lights went out in the house.

Wesley and I were huddled on the floor in the living room, just trying to do our best to keep ourselves alive for the next few hours.

RUMBLE. . .CLAPBOOM!

"Do you know what that sound is?" Rachel asked in her Witch voice.

That voice always creeped me out. But it made sense since her mom is a Witch.

"That's the sound of the Ender-zombie coming out to look for his dinner!"

RUMBLE. . .CLAPBOOM!

"HAHAHAHAHAHAHA!"

Wesley held me as tight as he could.

"Zumby, who's the ENDER-ZUMBY?" Wesley asked me in a scared voice.

"Rachel, please keep your stories to yourself. Can't you see you're creeping out the little kid!"

The truth was that I was getting creeped out.

I mean, after hearing about Harry O'Brien coming back from the dead to fight Steve and all the other crazy stuff that had been happening, I wouldn't doubt it if there was some creepy Enderman-zombie monster looking for some unsuspecting zombie to eat.

"Do you want to know who the Ender-zombie is?" Rachel creepily asked.

"Mmm-hmmm," Wesley and I said.

"Well, it was on a night like this that an unsuspecting young Zombie got lost and ended up in a cave to try to get dry. But what he didn't know was that the cave was the home of Ned, the Zombie flesh-eating Enderman!"

"HAHAHAHAHAHAHA!"

RUMBLE. . .CLAPBOOM!

"AAAAHHHHHHHHH!" Wesley and I screamed.

I wanted to tell Rachel to stop talking, but I couldn't move my mouth. I was frozen in utter terror.

"You see, one day in school, Ned, the Enderman, was dared to eat Zombie flesh and once he got a taste of it he couldn't stop himself from eating it. The cravings got so strong that he started having dreams of eating his Zombie classmates, Zombie neighbors, and his Zombie friends. So he ran away to the caves so that he wouldn't hurt anybody else."

GULP!

"So, this unsuspecting young Zombie that was trying to get out of the rain did not know that he was seeking refuge in the home of Ned, the Zombie Flesh-eating Enderman. Until it was too late!"

"HAHAHAHAHAHAHA!"

RUMBLE. . .CLAPBOOM!

"All the stories say is that the last thing the young Zombie saw were those big purple eyes just staring at him through the darkness. And before he knew it, Ned the Enderman was right next to him!"

"HAHAHAHAHAHAHA!"

RUMBLE. . .CLAPBOOM!

Seriously? Do we really need the laugh? I thought to myself. *I think Wesley already needs a diaper change. And if I had a diaper, I would too.*

"And as Ned the Enderman got closer, the Zombie lured Ned outside into the rain."

"AAARRRRGGGGGHHHH!!!!! Ned yelled as the water burned his Enderman skin like acid."

RUMBLE. . .CLAPBOOM!

"AAAAHHHHHHHHH!" Wesley and I screamed again.

"You see, what Ned the Enderman didn't know was that this scared Zombie that sought shelter in the cave was not really an innocent Zombie that had gotten lost. . .Instead, it was none other than the Enderman-eating and Zombie-eating Ender-zombie!"

"HAHAHAHAHAHAHA!"

"And as Ned lay there paralyzed by the rain, the Ender-zombie stood over him and let out a laugh. . ."

"HEHEHEHEHEHEHE!"

RUMBLE. . .CLAPBOOM!

"AAAAHHHHHHHHH!" Wesley and I screamed again.

"And they never heard from Ned the Enderman ever again."

Yeah, I definitely need a diaper change.

"So, when you hear the rain and the thunder, like it is out tonight, just know that the Enderzombie is out there and he is looking for his next meal. And you could be it!"

DING DONG!

"AAAAAAAAHHHHHHHHH-UUUHHHHH!"

FLUMP!

The last thing I remember was the Enderzombie hovering over me, smiling. . .then everything went black.

Thursday

When I woke up this morning, I expected to be moving around inside the stomach of the Ender-zombie.

Or, I expected all my zombie limbs to be half eaten because I figured it would take a few meals to get me down.

So, I tried not to open my eyes.

"Hi, Zumby!"

I knew that voice, but I knew it couldn't be Wesley. I was sure the Ender-zombie just popped him into his mouth like a snack.

"Zumby, open your eyes!"

So, I slowly opened my eyes and Wesley was standing over me. Then my mom walked into my room.

83

"Zombie, I hope you had a good sleep, but you need to get up for school," my mom said. "It's nighttime already."

Was it all a dream?

Oh, man, I've got to stop eating those spicy flavored booger snacks. But then I looked over at my computer and there was a sticky-note with the words, "Play Me."

So I turned on my computer and there was a maze game.

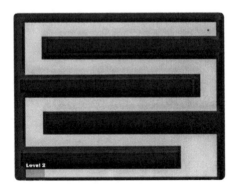

It was kind of easy; you just had to get the little ball through the maze without touching the walls. It started getting harder, so I had to really concentrate.

Also, it was getting hard to see so I had to get up real close to see the little ball.

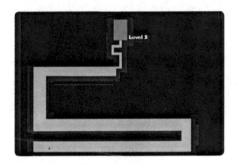

I was really good, but the mazes kept getting harder.

I almost had the ball through the final parts of the maze. . .

Just a little more and I was done. . .

Almost there. . .

"HAHAHAHAHAHAHA!"

"AAAAHHHHHHHHH!"

SPLATTT!

Oh man. . .

I think I need another diaper change.

At the end of the game, it said. . .

'Don't mess with me or I'm coming for you.'

Signed – R.P. – A.K.A. The Ender-Zombie.

Then everything went black. . .

Friday

I woke up again, and it was Friday.

I found out later, I missed a whole day of school because I fainted and wouldn't wake up.

My mom was going to take me the Witch Doctor because she thought I ate those berries in the garden again. But, I finally woke up this morning.

Man, I need to stay as far away from Rachel as possible.

That Wither skeleton is real poison in my life, I thought.

So, I went to school today trying to get back to my normal routine.

But every time I walked down the school hall everybody was snickering and laughing.

"Hey, what's everybody laughing at?" I asked the guys.

"You haven't seen it yet, have you?" Skelly asked me.

"I think we should show him," Slimey said.

"Show me what?"

The guys took me to the library to one of the computer terminals.

Then they brought up Noob-Tube.

"Zombie, just remember, no matter what you see, we're still your friends," Creepy said.

Then they played it.

". . .So when you hear the rain and the thunder like it is out tonight, just know that the Ender-zombie is out there and he is looking for his next meal!"

DING DONG!

"AAAAHHHHHHHHHUUUHHHHH!"
FLUMP!

What the what?!!!!

"Yeah, man. And it gets worse," Skelly said, clicking on the next video.

". . .Oh, a sticky note on my computer. . .Play Me? I wonder if my Mom got me a new game. . . Oh, a maze. . . I love mazes! I can beat this. . .That's easy. . .Uh oh, it's getting harder, huh? But I can still beat this. . .Just a little bit more. . .almost there. . .I'm totally gonna win this. . ."

"HAHAHAHAHAHAHA!"

"AAAAHHHHHHHHHH!"

SPLATT!

UUUHHHHHHHH!!! FLUMP!

What the what?!!!

"Yeah, man. It's gone viral. I think everybody in the whole school saw it," Skelly said.

"My cousin at Greendale High School said that it went viral in his school too," Slimey said. "I think it's gone viral everywhere."

Then I looked at the computer screen. . .

THE NOOB OF THE MONTH AWARD GOES TO ZACK ZOMBIE. WAY TO GO, NOOB!

Then they started playing the NOOB AND PROUD theme song.

"WWWWWAAAAAHHHHH!!!!!!"

"Don't worry, Zombie, I don't think Carrie saw it," Creepy said.

"Uh, yeah she saw it," Skelly said. "Look who nominated Zombie as Noob of the month."

"DARIUS FLENDERMAN!!!"

"Yeah, man. You know if he saw it, then everybody saw it in like twelve biomes."

WWWWWAAAAAHHHHH!!!!!!

UUUHHHHHHH!!! FLUMP!

Saturday

I woke up to a big nose with a mole on it.

It seems my mom finally called the Witch Doctor to check me out.

"Doctor, is it serious?"

"Mrs. Zombie, your son is fine. I think he just has a case of Z.M.D."

"Z.M.D.! What is that?" I asked.

"Oh, just a case of Zombie Melo-Drama-itis. But he'll get over it. He just needs to stop taking himself too seriously and start having a little fun."

"Oh dear. I was so worried," my mom said.

After the Witch Doctor left, my mom came into my room.

"Son, don't scare me like that. . .or the Ender-zombie will get you! AAAAHHHHHHHHH!"

"Mom!

"Sorry, Zombie, but the video was really cute. I even sent it to all of our relatives back west."

"Seriously?!!!"

"Yes. They said they're kids are always humming your theme song. . .NOOB AND PROUD."

WWWWWAAAAAHHHHH!!!!!!

"It's OK, Zombie. . .you should be proud for being Noob."

WWWWWAAAAAHHHHH!!!!!!

"Your father and I are Noobs, and we've been Noobs for years."

94

WWWWWAAAAAHHHHH!!!!!!

"You come from a long line of Noobs."

WWWWWAAAAAHHHHH!!!!!!

"But, anyway, get some rest, my little Noob"

Something tells me I don't think my mom knows what a Noob is.

So now the whole world thinks I'm a Noob.

That's it, my life is over.

I think I'm going to go live in an abandoned cave like Ned the Enderman.

Maybe the Ender-Zombie would just eat me and take me out of my misery.

Then I heard the doorbell downstairs.

"Hi, Creepy. Hi, Ellie," my mom said. "Yes, my little Noob is upstairs getting rest. Go right up."

Oh, brother!

"Hey, Zombie, how are you feeling?" Creepy asked.

"Terrible. The whole world thinks I'm a Noob, and now my life is over."

"Tee, hee," Carrie said. "Zombie, I've seen you play. You're not a Noob. I think you're really good."

"Then why did I get kicked out of Me-Tube? They said I was a Noob and should come back when my skills are better."

"That's weird," Ellie said. "The only time they ever kick somebody off Me-Tube is when someone accuses them of cheating."

"Seriously?"

"You know, I could find out if that's what happened to you," Ellie said. "Where's your computer?"

Then Ellie jumped on my computer as me and Creepy looked at her just whip through screen after screen with her mad computer hacking skills.

Clickety, clack, clickety, clack.

"Hey, Ellie, how come you don't play Minecraft anymore?" I asked her. "You were like, the best."

"It stopped being fun anymore. Especially when kids were getting really mean toward Noobs. It really bothered me, you know. Everybody's a Noob sometime. I just thought we should help Noobs and not put them down. So, I quit playing Minecraft."

"Whoa," I said.

"And that's when I started Noob-Tube."

"What the what?!!! You own Noob-Tube?!!!"

"Yeah, and I make a lot of money from it too. I'm too busy making money right now to play Minecraft anymore."

"Whoa!"

Clickety, clack, clickety, clack.

"Here it is. Somebody complained that you were using hacks to win all your games. They even showed a video of you beating one of the top players. The person who accused you said that there was no way you could've gotten so good so quick."

"Seriously?!!!"

"Yup. And the person who accused you was. . ."

Clickety, clack, clickety, clack.

"ScreamingPhoenix115."

"Who's that?"

"Well, nobody knows. . .except I wasn't the gaming champion for three years in a row for nothing."

Clickety, clack, clickety, clack.

"ScreamingPhoenix115's real name is. . ."

Clickety, clack, clickety, clack.

"You got to be kidding me!" Ellie said.

"Who is it?!! Who is it?!!"

"Darius Flenderman."

"What the what?!!!"

"Yeah, I've played ScreamingPhoenix115 in a lot of games and I beat him every time. I even caught him cheating, and I told him that if he didn't stop I would let everybody know he was cheating."

"Are you kidding me?"

"And once I stopped playing, he became the champion Minecraft player instead of me. But I bet he's still up to his old tricks. . .It's probably how he became champ."

Then I got an idea.

"Hey, Ellie, do you remember how he was cheating? Do you think you can teach me how to beat him?"

"I sure can," Ellie said. "But only if you promise to do something for me when all this is over."

Uh, oh. This is not going to be good.

"Uh, OK. I promise."

So, Ellie, Creepy and me spent the entire day practicing to beat Darius.

I still wasn't sure what Ellie wanted me to do, but I would do anything to beat Darius and show everybody that I wasn't a Noob.

Anything!

The next online gaming match was tomorrow night, and I was going to be ready.

Look out, Darius, here I come!

Sunday

I couldn't believe it!

It was the most amazing Minecraft PVP tournament ever!

I mean Darius was good. Really good.

But thanks to Ellie, I was able to anticipate all of his cheats and take him down!

He didn't even know what hit him.

I could tell he was really mad because Ellie told me that he sent in a lot of complaints to Me-Tube, Noob-Tube and all the other tubes, telling them that I was cheating.

But Ellie fixed him good.

She sent in a clip of Darius's playing and showed how he was cheating.

Darius got banned from all the Tubes in like twelve biomes!

Not to mention, he got banned from every server in the entire Minecraft Overworld.

So technically, now I'm the reigning Minecraft PVP Champ for miles around.

And thanks to Ellie, I can now get my Me-Tube account back.

"Congratulations, Zombie!" Creepy said as he and Ellie came into my room to congratulate me.

"Yeah, thanks so much, you guys! Especially you, Ellie. I couldn't have done it without you."

"Anytime, Zombie," Ellie said.

"No more Noob-Tube for me! Me-Tube here I come!"

"Hey, Zombie, remember that favor you said you would do for me after all this was over?" Ellie said with a really strange smile on her face.

"Yeeeaaaah. . ." I said, feeling really nervous.

Oh man. . .I think I'm in real trouble. . .

Monday

Well, I beat Darius.

And I got my Me-Tube account back.

But guess what?

I'm still a Noob.

Why?

Well, let's just say that I am the most popular Noob on Noob-Tube, thanks to Ellie.

That's because she made me make a video singing the NOOB AND PROUD song after beating Darius Flenderman.

She said it would empower Noobs everywhere to stand up and be proud to be Noobs, and to feel good about their Noob status.

She was right.

Now kids all around Noob-Tube are posting videos saying, "I'm a Noob and I'm Proud!"

They even had some kids on Me-Tube doing it too.

I even saw some kids outside wearing NOOB AND PROUD T-shirts.

Yeah, Ellie made them and now she's making more money than ever.

That's because now Noob-Tube is even bigger than every other Tube online.

It's even bigger than InstaScram, Critter, and Face-Mob Combined.

And my NOOB AND PROUD video is on the first page for the world to see.

So now, I'm going to be a Noob. . .forever.

Figures. . .

Tuesday

Today, we spent a few hours after school decorating the gym for the Dance Party.

Carrie was there looking tall, thin, and beautiful as usual.

I even saw Darius there.

Yeah, it seems like Darius' mom and dad heard he was cheating and made him do community service to help him get his act together.

Yeah, I didn't buy it either.

I actually heard there were a bunch of kids at school who were mad at Darius for cheating, and he didn't want to go home alone without Carrie.

What a Noob. . .

Anyway, since I was so popular now, I thought now was the time for me to ask Carrie to be my date for the Dance Party.

But before I asked her, I needed to practice my cool voice.

"Hey, Carrie, are you part Witch? Cause I think I'm under your spell."

Naw, naw, that won't work.

"Hi, Carrie. I must be standing in gravel because I'm falling for you!"

Nah!

"Hey, Carrie, are you from the Nether? Because I think you're out of this world."

All of a sudden, Carrie saw me staring at her from across the gym.

"AAAAHHHHHHHHH!" she yelled.

And then she disappeared.

"Dude, did Carrie catch you staring at her again?" Skelly asked.

"Uh. . .yeah. I couldn't help it. She just looked so good with her long arms and long legs and big head and purple eyes, and. . ."

"You know they say that stalking is a sign of intelligence," Creepy said. "Most famous mobs were stalkers at a young age. At least that's what they say in my family."

I just looked at Creepy.

"Aw, man! That was my ride," Darius said with a mad look on his face.

I knew Darius was mad at me for beating him at Minecraft PVP. But now I could tell he was really mad.

Then he started going crazy and teleporting all over the gym.

"You just wait, Zombie, you're gonna get yours. . .and soon!" he said. Then he disappeared.

Aw great! Not only does Carrie think I'm a stalker and hate me, now I have a crazy Enderman plotting to get his revenge on me.

Man, what else could go wrong?

Wednesday

"**Z**ombie, the babysitter will be here any minute now!"

WHAT?!!!!

NONONONONONONONO!

"Zombie, I'm sorry but your father and I need to go the PTA meeting to prepare for the Dance Party that's coming up at your school a few days."

"MOM, please don't leave me with her. . .She's a Witch and she going to eat me!"

"Zombie, is your Z.M.D. acting up again?" my mom asked with a chuckle.

"Seriously. Mom, she's crazy!"

113

"Zombie, please don't talk about her that way. She's just a girl who needs a lot of support and encouragement."

"Mom, she doesn't need encouragement. She needs a straightjacket!"

"Wow, Zombie, you look sick. Have you been eating those berries in the garden again?"

"Yeah, yeah, Mom, my stomach hurts. Uuuurrggghhh! I ate a whole bunch of those berries, and I feel like I'm dying!"

"Well, I guess we can't have the babysitter coming when you're sick," my mom said. "You go upstairs and get into bed and I will make you some mushroom stew. That should help you sweat out the berries."

Man, mushroom stew is like the nastiest thing on the planet. I'm either going to sweat out the berries or bleed them out of my eyes.

But, it's totally worth it. I won't last another day with that witch, Rachel Patella, babysitting me again.

DING, DONG!

Oh, man, there she is now.

"Oh, hi," I heard my mom say from downstairs. "Yeah, I'm sorry, Zombie got really sick from eating those berries in the garden again. I think it's a puberty thing. Like that mole he grew on his. . ."

What the what?!!!

"Sure," she continued. "I'll tell him you said hi. Goodbye, Carrie."

"CARRIE?!!!!!"

I ran downstairs as fast as I could, but by the time I opened the door Carrie's dad's car was driving away.

Man, I missed my chance!

"You're not sick, are you?!!! my mom yelled. "I have a good mind to ground you for a month. But your father and I still need to go to that PTA meeting tonight."

"Mom, I'm sorry. It's just. . ."

"Don't I'm sorry me. You just head back up to your room right now."

"Now, who can I call this late in the day to watch the kids?" I heard my mom ask my dad as I was walking up the stairs. "I know, I'll call Rachel. She's probably available."

RACHEL!!!!!!

WWWAAAAHHHHHH!!!!!!!

Thursday

Well...

You're probably wondering what happened last night with Rachel...right?

Yeah...Me too...

I can't remember anything from last night.

All I remember is Mom calling Rachel, and Rachel telling her how excited she was to come over.

Then the doorbell rang, Rachel walked in and then everything when black.

I think it was so traumatic that I blocked it out.

The only thing I'm still trying to figure out is how I got this scar where one of my kidneys use to be.

Man, where is that kidney?

I always seem to misplace those things.

Well, the Dance Party is in a few days.

So it's my last chance to ask Carrie to be my date.

I better do it today or somebody else might ask her instead of me.

I know, I'll call her on the phone.

RING!

"Hello?"

"Hey, what's going on?"

"Nothing, what's going on with you?"

"Nothing, what's going on with you?"

"Nothing, what's going on with you?"

"Hey, I wanted to call Carrie and ask her to be my date for the party tomorrow, but I don't know what to say."
"Dude, that's bold," Skelly said.

"I need some help with some really cool line. . .like from a movie or something."

"Oh, man, I got a good one. I saw it in a movie about this really cool spy named Dirk Craftly—but you gotta say it with a really tough, manly, scary voice. Girls dig that."

Then Skelly gave me the really good line from the Dirk Craftly movie that I could use to ask Carrie to the Dance Party.

"Awesome, man, thanks. I'm going to call her right now."

Once I got the courage, and after I practiced my really tough, manly, scary voice, I dialed Carrie's number.

RING!

"Hello?"

"Hey, baby, you remind me of my appendix because something inside me is saying I should take you out."

"Who is this?!!! Harold! There's a stalker on the phone!"

Oh, man. . .

"Who is this?!!!" Carrie's dad said, taking the phone. "I don't know who you are, mister, but if you scare my wife like that ever again, I will find you and I will end you!"

"Uh, I'm sorry, Mr. Flenderman. . ."

Oh, man, I forgot to stop my scary voice!

"Cough, cough. . .I mean, sorry, Mr. Flenderman. Is Carrie home?"

"Carrie? What do you want with my daughter, you weirdo?!!!"

"Uh. . .this is Zack. Lionel's son."

"Lionel? Oh. . .Zombie! I didn't recognize you. Going through puberty, huh? Yeah, I remember the days. . .I'll get Carrie for you."

Then I heard Mr. and Mrs. Flenderman in the background.

"Harold, who is it?" Mrs. Flenderman asked.

"It's Lionel's son, calling for Carrie. Where is she? Carrie!!! You got a phone call!"

"Are you sure that's a boy?" Mrs. Flenderman said. "It sounded like a stalker to me."

"Oh, Edith, the boy's going through puberty. They all sound like that."

121

Rustle. . .Rustle. . .

"Daddy, I got it! Hello?" Carrie said in her sweet, amazing voice.

"Hi, Carrie, it's Zack. . .Uh. . ."

"Hi, Zack. What's up? I heard you were sick. Your mom said you had a mole or something."

"Uh. . .yeah. . .um…that cleared up. . .but I wanted to ask you something. . ."

"Sure, what's up?"

Then I put on my tough, manly, scary voice again. . .

"Hey, baby, you remind me of my appendix because something inside me is saying I should take you out."

"What? Zack, what's wrong with your voice?"

"Cough, cough. . .Nothing, um. . .I wanted to ask you if you would be my date for the Mob Middle School Dance Party?"

"Oh. . ."

Silence.

It felt like I was sitting there waiting for like a thousand years.

"Sure. I'd love to. . ."

"No, I understand. . .I know you're busy and. . .wait, what?"

"I said I'd love to go. Except, I still have to help out with the party in between dances if that's OK with you. But sure, I'd love to go."

What the what?!!!!

She said yes!!!!

I'm the Man! I'm the Man!

Mmph! Mmph! Mmph! Mmph!

(That's me doing my happy dance, by the way. . .)

Yeah!

Superstah!

"Zombie, are you still there?"

"Uh. . .um. . .yeah, I'm still here."

"OK, I'll meet you there at six o'clock because I have to be there early to help with decorations."

"Yeah. . .that sounds great."

"OK. . .bye."

"Bye. . ."

Wow! I've got a date with the most awesome girl in all of Minecraft.

Man, Skelly was right. That line worked like a charm.

From now on, Dirk Craftly, you're my new hero!

Friday

Well, tomorrow is the Mob Middle School eighth grade Dance Party!

But, more importantly, tomorrow is my big date with Carrie Flenderman!

So I need to get ready.

Now, I wanted a really cool haircut.

So I asked my dad to take me to the Zombie barber.

Except everybody at the barber shop gave me a weird look when I told them I wanted to look like Dirk Craftly.

Except for one guy. I really thought he got what I was saying.

Until, after he finished, I realized he thought I said Dirk Ghastly.

So now I look like a Ghast and a Zombie had a baby and then they dropped him a few times.

It's a good thing this stuff scrapes off.

But I finished my Dirk Craftly costume, though, and it looks sweet!

It makes me look cool and smooth, hairy and manly all at the same time.

But, most importantly, it lets me move around on the dance floor so I can show off my sweet moves.

Yeah, I know. You probably didn't know that I had sweet moves.

But, oh yeah. . .I do. Let me show you what I got!

I usually start with a little Zombie Overbite. . .

Mmph! Mmph! Mmph! Mmph!

(That's me doing the Zombie Overbite, by the way. . .)

Then I jump in with the Zombie Slam. . .

Mmph! Boom! Chicka! Boom! Mmph!
Mmph! Mmph!

Then I switch to some floor action with my favorite Zombie breakdance move. . .

Then, of course, I throw in a little Zombie
Robot. . .

And then I end it like a gangsta. . .

AWWWYEAAHHBBOOYYEEEE!!!

Oh, man, Carrie's gonna love it!

I can see us now. . .

DIRK (In his manly, hairy voice): "Hey, Carrie, it's me, Dirk Craftly. . ."

CARRIE (In her cute, girly voice): "Oh, Dirk, you're so amazing!"

DIRK: "Hey, Carrie, did you just fart? Because you just blew me away. . .He. . .He. . ."

CARRIE: "Oh, Dirk, you just say the nicest things!"

DIRK: "Hey, Carrie, you know, my love for you is like diarrhea. I just can't hold it in. . .He. . .He. . ."

CARRIE: "Oh, Dirk, you make me feel so special!"

DIRK: "Hey, Carrie. . ."

KNOCK, KNOCK.

134

"Hey, Zombie, are you getting ready for your big date tomorrow?" my mom said with her mom face.

Oh, brother. Just when I was really getting my manly Dirk Crafty on. . .

"What is it, Mom?"

"Nothing. . .I just wanted to see how much my Zombaby has grown up. . .Sniffle, sniffle," my mom said with water coming out of her eye sockets.

"Aww, Mom, it's just a dance!"

"I know, I know. Well, anyway. . .I brought you some cream to cover up that mole. . ."

"Mom!"

Man, talk about embarrassing. My mom gets all weird like that whenever I talk about girls.

Moms are so weird.

Dad, on the other hand, really gets it.

"Hey, son, going on your date tomorrow? Well, have fun."

Yeah, he really gets it.

Saturday

Well, I convinced my mom and dad to drop me off a few blocks from the school.

I couldn't be seen going into my eighth grade school dance with my parents.

Plus, me and the guys planned to meet together and all come in together like a posse.

And parents are definitely not part of the posse.

When we all walked in, the place looked awesome.

All the hard work we put in decorating really paid off.

The dance this year was called, "Night at the Abandoned Mineshaft."

They even brought in a real minecart to make it look more realistic.

Not only that, but the party had mountains of food.

I mean it had mountains of Skittles, mountains of M&Ms, and they even had a fountain of Mountain Dew.

But the best part, they had tables and tables full of all kinds of cake!

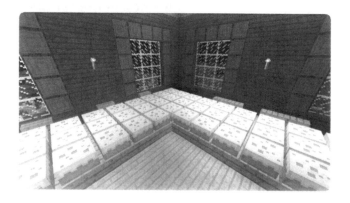

When we looked around, for some reason all the boys were on one side of the gym and all the girls were on the totally other side.

It looked like boys against girls volleyball night.

"You should go over there," one of the Skelton boys whispered to Emory the Creeper, daring him to cross the chasm that stood before us.

"Alright, I will," Emory said.

All the other Mob boys just stared in hopeful anticipation as the brave creeper stepped out into the abyss.

About a few steps into his epic journey, all we heard was "TSSSSSSSSSS."

It's a good thing there were some parents there.

They escorted poor Emory outside.

Good for us.

BOOM!

Not so good for the parents. . .

Then from across the room, I could see Carrie Flenderman as she teleported from place to place making sure the decorations were all in place.

"Dude, don't stare. . ." Creepy said. "You don't want to ruin your big chance with Carrie."

"Yeah, be cool, man," Skelly said. "Remember, you're Dirk Craftly, superspy."

"Oh, yeah, that's right. I need to be coooooooool."

"Dude, what's wrong with your voice?" Slimely asked.

Anyway, I decided to make my move.

Well, wouldn't you know it, right before
I went over to Carrie to say hi, Darius
Flenderman stepped in front of me.

Oh, man, what now?

"Hey, Zombie, I just wanted to say. . . I'm
sorry for the other day," Darius said.

Even though I wasn't really listening because
I was too busy looking at Carrie teleport
around in her cute way, I heard that last part.

"Seriously?"

"Yeah, man, no hard feelings," Darius said.
"Shake?"

Then he stuck out his hand, or arm. . .(You
can't really tell with an Enderman), and I
shook it.

Then, Carrie teleported to another side of the
gym to finish her decorations.

141

Aw, man! Missed her.

"Hey, Zombie, Carrie wanted me to tell you that she needed your help with the confetti," Darius said.

"Confetti? What confetti?"

"Well, in a few minutes, Carrie is going to get on stage and welcome everyone to the dance and she needs you to pull this rope and it'll tip a bucket that will drop confetti all over the place."

"Why me?" I asked Darius, not sure if I could trust him.

"She said you're the only one she trusts to do it right," he said.

Whoa. Carrie thinks I'm the only one she can trust? Wow, she must really like me.

"OK, I'll do it!"

Then Darius showed me where to stand and he handed me the rope.

I saw the bucket right above the stage, and I was wondering how all the confetti was going to get on everyone.

I'm sure Carrie's got it all planned out; she's really smart, I thought.

"So, in a few minutes, when Carrie yells out, 'Welcome eighth grade class to the Mob Middle School Dance!' you just pull the rope, OK?" Darius said.

"OK," I said, wondering why Darius looked all sweaty.

So I waited there for about ten minutes and saw Carrie get on stage.

Oh, man, Carrie is so going to see that I am a Zombie she can trust. Yeah, Dirk Craftly the manliest, hairiest and most trustworthy Zombie there is. . ."

"AND NOW, FOR WHAT WE'VE ALL BEEN WAITING FOR. . ."

Oh, man, I better get ready!

"WELCOME EIGHTH GRADE CLASS TO THE MOB MIDDLE SCHOOL DANCE!"

So I pulled on the rope as hard as I could.

Except. . .

Instead of confetti, water came pouring down.

I could see it right now in slow motion. . .I pulled the rope. . .the bucket tipped. . .water poured out of the bucket. . .down. . .down. . .down. . .Splash!

Until it landed all over Carrie.

Suddenly, all the music stopped and everyone just stared at Carrie.

Then they all looked over at me because
Darius took the spotlight and shined it in my
direction.

"HUH! GASP! OMZ!" everyone said.

All of a sudden, Carrie started making these
strange noises.

It started out as low grunts and then squeals,
and then finally. . .

SSSHHHRRRIIIIIEEEEEKKKKKK!!!!!

Suddenly, the torches on the walls started flickering on and off.

Next thing, we heard all the doors of the gym slam shut.

Then out of nowhere cake started levitating in the air.

And all of a sudden. . .

SPLAT!

SPLOOSH!

SPLUNK!

Everybody started getting smashed in the face with cake!

Enderman, Creepers, Shulkers went crazy and were teleporting, levitating and exploding.

Skeletons started shooting arrows to try to keep from being smashed with cake.

Zombie's were grunting and groaning.

147

And Slimes were bouncing all around the place.

It was crazy!

Nobody knew what to do.

And I know this sounds crazy, but for some reason I knew exactly what Dirk Craftly would do.

He would go over there and kiss Carrie, and she would totally fall in love with Dirk and then she would totally chillax.

So I knew I had to make my move.

"Zombie," Creepy asked me as we were hiding under a table, "what are you doing?"

"I need to kiss her," I said.

"Dude, you do know how crazy that sounds, right?" Skelly said.

"I know, that's why it's gonna work," I said in my Dirk Craftly voice.

"Dude, what's wrong with your voice?" Slimey asked me.

So as all the mob kids and parents were running for their lives, I ran toward Carrie.

It was really hard getting through the tornado of skittles, Mountain Dew, and cake.

But I made it through without getting smashed in the face.

Carrie saw me staring at her as I came closer and closer.

But, for some reason, this time she didn't teleport away.

So I got closer and closer.

Suddenly, I took a step and my left arm flew off.

Then I took another step and my right arm flew off.

Carrie was just too powerful.

But I was getting closer.

So then, I took another step and my Dirk Craftly hat flew off.

I finally got as close to her as I could. But I couldn't get close enough to plant one on her.

So, I just whispered in her ear in my manliest, hairiest, Dirk Craftly voice. . .

"Hey, baby, uh. . .if girls were boogers, I'd pick you first, chyea!"

Silence.

Tee. . .Tee. . .Teehee. . .Teeheehee. . .

All of a sudden, Carrie started laughing!

The good thing was that more she laughed the more the tornado of condiments started to die down.

"Hey, Carrie, is your middle name Google? Cause you've got everything I'm searching for."

"Ha. . .Ha. . .Hahahahaha. . .Hahahahahaha!"

I knew it, she couldn't resist the Dirk Craftly charm!

That's when I made my move.

SMOOCH!

"HUH?"

BAMF!

Next thing you know, Carrie teleported away.

Everybody came out of their hiding places to see if the coast was clear.

Except for Darius. He got stuck in the Minecart and got hit with so much cake and Mountain Dew that he looked like a snow man at a dog convention.

And as I looked out at the sea of mob kids covered in condiments, somebody started slow clapping.

Until the whole gym was clapping in happiness and excitement. And I stood proud because they knew that I, Dirk Zombie Craftly, was their hero. . .

. . .Actually, Skelly started slow clapping and nobody followed.

"Dude, you are such a loser," Rachel said as she rolled her eye sockets at him.

Sunday

I woke up this morning feeling like a new zombie.

I mean, besides not having arms, I just felt like I was the best thing since sliced Minecraft bread.

Not only did I save the school, but when I got home last night Carrie and her family came by to apologize.

And before Carrie left. . .she kissed me.

What can I say. . .

I'm the Man! I'm the Man!

Mmph! Mmph! Mmph! Mmph!

(That's me doing my happy dance, by the way. . .but with no arms.)

Yeah!

Superstah!

Anyway, my mom got me some spare arms from the basement, which was cool.

Except I think one belonged to a sailor Zombie 'cause it had a tattoo with the word "Mom" on it.

Yeah, I told you moms were weird.

The other arm belonged to a kid that really liked picking his nose.

I know because of the really long pinky nail.

Comes in really handy, though.

I'm rebuilding my booger collection.

Monday

Today, I went to go see Steve to see how he was holding up with the upcoming death match with Herobrine.

CLAPBOOM!

That is so strange when that happens. . .

Then, I started thinking. Man, that must really be tough. I can't even imagine what it must feel like to have the safety of the whole Overworld on your shoulders.

But if anyone can handle it, it's Steve.

That guy is the bravest human, or Mob, I have ever met.

So if anyone is going to save the Overworld from utter destruction, it's going to be Steve.

When I got to Steve's house, I just found his suitcase outside of his house.

So I walked inside and saw Steve getting ready to leave.

"Uh. . .where you going, Steve?"

"Oh. . .uh. . .I'm just taking a little vacation. . .for like the next one hundred years."

"Seriously?"

"Yeah, man," Steve said. "I can't beat him. Herobrine is too tough. He's got magic powers, and all I can do is punch a tree."

CLAPBOOM!

"See!"

"What about punching one tree ten thousand times like your 'San Soo' said?"

"You mean 'sensei.' And his name is Spruce Lee and I saw it on television, OK. I'm no ninja."

156

Oh, man. If Steve can't beat. . .uh. . ."H," then it's going to mean that "H" is going to destroy the Overworld. And I'll never get a chance to experience life with Carrie as my girlfriend.

"Steve, you gotta fight him, man. You're the only one who can.

"I don't know, man," Steve said. "Nice tattoo, by the way."

"Oh, thanks. . .but if you can't fight him, what are we going to do?"

Steve looked at me for a minute and then dropped his suitcase.

"Yeah, you're right!" Steve said as he walked over and started punching the tree again.

"I guess if I have to die so that the rest of the Overworld could live, then so be it!"

Punch, punch, punch. . .

Wow, I can't let Steve die. He's like my best friend in the whole Overworld.

But what can I do?

As I said goodbye to Steve, I realized this might be the last week that I will ever see him again.

And that's when I realized what I needed to do.

I need to destroy the Wicked Witch of the Well, and hopefully that'll stop "H" from destroying Steve and the rest of the Overworld.

Yep, that's what I need to do.

Gulp!

Yep, uhhhh. . . that's what I need to do.

Tuesday

I finally found a posse to take with me to fight the Wicked Witch of the Well.

I asked a lot of people to come, but a lot of them gave me strange looks as soon as I mentioned the story of the Wicked Witch of the Well.

Or was it when I mentioned Dirk Craftly?

Eh, I couldn't tell.

Anyway, I asked I.P. Freely to come but I think he said he's still allergic to stupid.

Rajit was going to come, but he had some Shulker relatives who decided to float in at the last minute.

And I went to go ask Alex, but she was out of town at a Minecon conference.

So it was up to me, Skelly, Slimey, and Creepy to face the Wicked Witch of the Well all by ourselves.

We got together to come up with a plan, when Old Man Jenkins came by with his Zombie horse.

"What in tarnation are you kids up to now?" Old Man Jenkins asked.

"We're going to go destroy the Wicked Witch of the Well," I said.

Suddenly, Old Man Jenkins turned whiter than a Snow Golem at a milk convention.

"You're going where to do what?!!!!"

"We need to destroy the Wicked Witch of the Well," I said. Then I told him all about Herobrine and Steve and their death match.

CLAPBOOM!

160

"What in tarnation wuzzat?" Mr. Jenkins said, jumping out of his boots. "Well, anyway, if you're going to destroy the Witch, then the only chance you got is to fight her during the next full blood moon. Yessir, that's when she's at her weakest."

"Blood moon?!!!"

All of us just looked at each other.

"What's a blood moon?" Slimey asked hesitantly.

"That's when the moon turns blood red," he said. "It gets filled with the souls of all the dead that rise up to feed on the livin'."

"What the what?!!!!"

"I'm just kiddin'," he said. "The blood moon is a glitch that happens during every new Minecraft update."

"Whew!" we all said at the same time.

"So when's the next blood moon?" Slimey asked Mr. Jenkins.

"Uh, if my memory serves me right, the next one is Thursday night, October 12th, a few hours before midnight."

"Oh, man, that's cutting it really close, Zombie," Skelly said.

"Yeah. That means we need to get to the abandoned cave, climb down the well, find the Witch, destroy her without getting killed and get back just in time to help Steve, all within like three hours."

"Yep, that's about right," Mr. Jenkins said.

"Mr. Jenkins, do you want to come with us to fight the Wicked Witch of the Well? You also get an honorary membership into the Dirk Craftly Fan Club for a nominal fee."

Old Man Jenkins gave me a same strange look.

"Sorry, boys, I'm going to have to pass," he said. "Me and that old hag have crossed paths before. If I get hit by her poison again, I don't think I'll make it back this time."

Poison?

Gulp!

Me and the guys just looked at each other again.

"Zombie, are you sure we should do this? I mean, the Wicked Witch sounds really tough," Creepy said.

"We can do it, guys! We have to! Steve is depending on us!" I said, trying to rally the troops and keep their spirits up the way I thought Dirk Craftly would.

But the truth was I was scared. Really scared.

But I had to try.

I know Steve would, no matter what the odds.

So I have to, too.

So, Wicked Witch of the Well. . .Gulp!

Get ready, 'cause here we come!

Wednesday

Today me and the guys got together at the library to do some research about the Wicked Witch of the Well.

I really wish we hadn't, though. . .

Because everything we read made her sound scarier and scarier.

One website talked about how one time she was seen by a bunch of local villagers and mobs. And then a few days later, villagers and mobs started disappearing.

One zombie even wrote about his experience with the Wicked Witch after visiting the area surrounding the Abandoned Cave. . .

I am a photographer, I take many pictures of things, mostly villagers, mobs, caves, nature, etc. One day while driving around the area known as the Abandoned Cave, I saw a bridge. A very large "thing" was on top of it. The thing looked like a giant bird with bright red eyes. So I took a picture of it. As I researched it, I found out other people had seen it too. They called it the legend of the Wicked Witch of the Well.

A few weeks went by as I wondered about that strange creature. I even saw it in my dreams. Then one night, while I was shooting pictures of a dark and scary cave, I heard something that sounded like it was circling around me, flying. I looked up and all I could see were those red, scary eyes. I ran to my car and it followed. As I got back into town, somebody had a shirt on with this creature with those red scary eyes and it totally creeped me out.

On another occasion, I was driving on the highway at night and as I looked up in the sky I saw those red, scary eyes looking at me.

What was weird was that I was driving about seventy-five miles an hour and that thing was right on top of me, following my car. I pulled into a gas station to get gas and to change my underwear. As I was getting back into the car, I noticed huge scratch marks on top of my car. Then I drove home as fast as I could, hoping to never see that thing ever again.

I took two pictures of this creature, but I'm afraid to upload them because of what might happen to me. But I am uploading one to warn all the villagers and mobs around to stay as far away from this area as possible.

. . .Or the Wicked Witch will haunt you forever.

(Unfortunately, the anonymous photographer went missing shortly after he uploaded the photo below. Police are still investigating his whereabouts. If you hear something, please contact your local police station).

GULP!

After I read that, I gotta be honest. . .me and the guys almost chickened out.

Yep, we almost called the whole plan off.

But later that night, I went to go see Steve to wish him luck. And to let him know what a chicken I was.

But as I got closer to his house, I could see Steve punching that same tree over and over again.

I stood there for a while, just looking as Steve doing his best to keep us all safe.

That's when I knew, even though I might be scared, I've gotta do my part and help my best friend save the world.

So, I ran home and called the guys and inspired them to go out tomorrow to battle the Witch for the sake of Steve and all of Minecraft!

Yeah, really manly. . .I know.

Dirk Craftly would be so proud.

Thursday

So we all got ready to go find the Wicked Witch of the Well.

The most important thing we needed to do was destroy the Witch before Steve battled "HIM" tonight at midnight.

That meant we only had a few hours to find the Witch and dispatch her once and for all.

So me and the guys finally reached the Abandoned Cave and the well, which looked scarier than usual.

It was probably because we all knew we were there to meet the Wicked Witch of the Well.

And we weren't sure if we were even going to make it back or not.

"HAHAHAHAHAHAHA!"

"AAAAAHHHHHH!!!!"

We all yelled and just held onto each other while waiting to die.

"You guys are so easy," we heard a voice say.

"Wha. . .? RACHEL!"

Of course, it was Rachel. It had to be Rachel. I'm gonna die, and Rachel is going to be standing over me dancing on my bones.

"Rachel, what are you doing here?" Skelly asked with his puppy dog eyes and droopy-eyed look.

"You guys don't think you're gonna have all the fun, do you?" Rachel said. "Plus, I got my reasons for getting rid of the Wicked Witch of the Well."

"Really? What did she ever do to you?" Skelly asked.

Maybe it was because she felt sorry for us. Or maybe it was because she knew we were all going to die anyway. . .or maybe she just liked telling scaring stories. . .(Yeah, that was probably it). . .but Rachel started telling us about her history with old WWW.

"Well, the Wicked Witch of the Well's real name is Wanda Witch Hazel," she said. "I know because people in my family used to call her Aunt Wanda."

"Whoa!"

"I knew you were related to the Wicked Witch, I just knew it!" I said happily. Until Rachel gave me one of her dirty looks again for interrupting her story.

"Oh. . .sorry."

"Well, Aunt Wanda fell in love with a dashing and handsome young Wither Skeleton. But, unfortunately, the Wither Skeleton didn't feel the same way. You see he was in love with someone else. . .my mom!"

"HAHAHAHAHAHA!"

"Really, the cackling, again?"

"Anyway, Aunt Wanda grew so jealous that she conjured up a spell to make my dad into a hideous monster so that my mom would reject him and she could have him all to herself."

"Whoa!"

"But after she changed him, my mom's love for my dad was so strong that it didn't matter if he had three heads, she was going to love all of them."

"Whoa!"

"Aunt Wanda was so enraged that she went crazy and started attacking human villagers and even Minecraft Mobs. That is until they caught her and punished her for all eternity by throwing her down this well."

"Whoa!"

"So you see, I'm here to get my revenge for what she did to my dad. So even if I have to do it with you Noobs, nothing is going to stop me."

That was enough for me. Plus, I didn't even want to say no to Rachel. She might turn me into a three-headed monster or something.

And, not to mention that Rachel was the only one that brought rope so we could get down the well.

Slimey didn't really need the rope, though.

Slimes bounce, remember?

Well, we finally made it to the bottom of the well and it was dark. . .like pitch-black dark.

We felt our way around and found an entrance to a tunnel. As we walked through the tunnel we could see some lights that led to another big cave.

We all went through the tunnel until we made it to the end, where we walked into a big cave lit with torches.

The cave was big, with a crafting table on one wall and a big empty cauldron with a brewing stand next to it standing on the other wall. And in the middle of the cave was a big pot full of what looked like mushroom stew.

"Oh, man, I'm hungry," Slimey said.

"Don't touch it, man, that's probably a Mob stew full of all kinds of Creeper entrails, and ears and stuff," Creepy said.

"Eewww, really?" Rachel said giving Creepy the 'you are so weird' look. Then she went over and put her hand over the pot. "This is still warm so that means the Wicked Witch is close by."

"Wait. . .what?!!! we all said.

Suddenly, we heard a noise and we all just jumped up.

"What was that?!!! What was that?!!! What was that?!!!!" we all whispered and yelled at the same time.

"You guys need to calm down, it's just a cat," Rachel said.

Suddenly, a black cat walked up to us and began to hiss.

"HSSSSSS," the cat said.

"TSSSSSS," Creepy said back.

Creepy must've said something to the cat because the cat ran away quick.

"Way to go, Creepy!"

"Wuzzat?" Creepy said.

Then Rachel ran over to the wall, where there was a shelf full of different colored potions.

"This is what we need to destroy the Witch," Rachel said as she started grabbing bottles.

"What are these for?" I asked Rachel.

"Honestly, my brewing is a bit rusty," Rachel said. "My mom is more like a soccer Mom Witch instead of the wicked kind. She even got her mole removed with laser surgery."

"Seriously?!!"

"Yeah, you should consider it, Zombie. From what your mom told me, your mole is getting pretty big and hairy, right?"

"Aw, man!"

"Anyway, if I remember right, this potion is for fire resistance. And that is for healing. This one is for flying. And that one is for Noobs like you. . .it's called an Awkward Potion."

"Ha ha, funny," I said.

Then I saw a blue bottle with water that looked a little like the one Steve used to put the fire out at his house with when "H" torched it. I took a few to take to Steve for his battle with "HIM."

Then I saw a couple of green potion bottles.

"What's that?" I said as I reached for them.

"Don't touch those," Rachel said, slapping my hand. "I think those are the potions the Witch uses to poison mobs. . .that is, before she eats them."

Gulp!

Then Rachel grabbed a few of the green bottles as I walked over to the guys to see how they were doing.

As I was walking toward the guys, suddenly the torches went out.

"HAHAHAHAHAHAHA!"

"What the what?!!!" we all yelled, scared out of our wits.

"Hey, that's not funny, Rachel," I said.

Silence.

"Rachel?. . .Rachel?. . . "Hey, stop playing, OK?"

Then the lights instantly came back on.

"AAAAAAAHHHHH!!!!!"

Right in front of us was the ugliest old Witch I had ever seen, and she was huge. Like mutant huge. And she had glowing red eyes.

And she had Rachel and was covering her mouth with her big, meaty, hairy hand. She was also holding one of the green splash potion bottles in her other hand.

Me and the guys were just frozen solid in fear.

Rachel looked like she was trying to say something or trying to hurl. But the Witch's nasty hand was covering her mouth.

Man, if she put that hand over my mouth I'd probably want to hurl too.

Then, Rachel tried to roll her eyes but since she didn't have any I couldn't understand what she was trying to say.

Suddenly, the Witch threw her splash potion at me and the guys and we all jumped away from it.

We crashed into the shelf with all the other potions, and the whole shelf came crashing down.

I thought we had escaped, but suddenly Skelly, Slimey and Creepy started falling to the floor one at a time.

Then I thought I was the only one who escaped, but all of a sudden, I started feeling weaker and weaker.

Finally, Rachel got her mouth free and yelled.

"Throw the potion!"

I think Rachel forgot that I didn't pick up the green potion. And the only potion bottle I had was the water bottle.

So before I collapsed to the floor, I threw the water bottle at the Witch.

KRESH!

The water bottle hit her right in the face. But it was only water, so I knew it was useless.

I hit the floor, but not before seeing Rachel break free.

"You did it, Zombie!"

"Wha. . .?"

Then I looked over at the Witch, who looked like she had something stuck in her throat.

She finally yelled out. . .

"NOOOOOOOOO. . .I'M MELTING!"

Rachel grabbed a pink potion of healing bottle that wasn't broken and gave some to me and the guys.

We all started feeling better.

"I'M MELTING, I'M MELTING, I'M MELTING!" the Witch yelled. "I'LL COME BACK FOR YOU!!!. . .I PROMISSRRRGGG. . ."

Then all that was left was a puddle in the middle of the floor.

"Ewww. . .Witch juice," Slimey said.

"Man, I knew mobs aren't supposed to take baths, but I didn't know it was this bad," I said.

"Yeah, Aunt Wanda was allergic to water. I think it's because her father was the Ender-zombie."

"Seriously?!!!"

Rachel just smiled at me with her usual sinister smile.

"So, since the Wicked Witch is gone does this mean Steve is safe?" Skelly asked.

"I don't know, but we better grab the rest of the potion bottles just in case," I said.

There were only two potions left that hadn't broken. One potion of fire resistance and one potion of healing.

"Hey, what time is it?" I asked the guys.

"Oh, man, its fifteen minutes till midnight," Creepy said.

"Let's head back and see if we can help Steve," I said.

So we ran out of the cave, and ran as fast as we could to Steve's house.

Oh, man. . .I hope we're not too late.

Friday – October 13th
12:15 am

We ran as fast as we could.

But I think it was too late.

As we were getting closer to Steve's house, all we could see was a giant crater where Steve's house used to be.

"Zombie I think we're too late," Creepy said, running on his little feet. . .or hands. . .or whatever those things are.

But when we got to the edge of the crater, we looked down and saw Steve on the ground and "H" hovering over him about to strike the final blow.

"STINKY!" I yelled.

CLAPBOOM!

It was enough to get Herobrine's attention and distract him for a second before he went back to pronounce Steve his death sentence.

"And you know what, Steve?" Herobrine said. "After I destroy you, I'm going to destroy your friends too."

"What?!!! You promised you would leave them alone, cough. . .cough," Steve said.

"Eh. . .what can I say. . .I'm not a man anymore, so I don't have to keep my word. I AM A GOD! HAHAHAHAHAHA!"

As Herobrine was busy admiring himself, I grabbed one of the last few potion bottles from my pocket.

"Now, I will finally get my revenge!" Herobrine said as he was about to deliver the final blast that would totally annihilate Steve.

KRESH!

"BOOOM!"

Herobrine unleashed a huge fiery blast at Steve, and we all of us just stood there with our mouths open, powerless to do anything to help him.

Suddenly, as the smoke cleared. . .

"STEVE!!!!!"

Steve was still alive, untouched by the fire blast.

The fire resistance potion worked! Though, honestly, I wasn't sure which potion I threw at him.

Then Rachel threw the potion of healing at Steve and he stood up.

"WHAT! THIS IS IMPOSSIBLE! HOW CAN THIS BE?!!!"

"Goes to show you, Stinky, I have a superpower you will never have. . ."

"And what's that?" Herobrine asked sneeringly.

"My friends!"

CLAPBOOM!

Then Steve pulled his arm back farther than I had ever seen him pull it ever. And then he thrust it forward with all his might.

Suddenly. . .

BAABBBBLLLLLLAAAAAAAMMMMM!!!!!!

POP!

Herobrine just stood there, staring at Steve. . .not really sure what just happened.

Then when the smoke cleared, all we could see was a pair of bony legs running all around the place.

The rest of Herobrine's Skeleton just shot off in different directions.

Next thing we heard was. . .

PSSSSSSSSSSS.

STEVE!!!! You did it!!!!!

We all ran over to Steve and gave him a big high five.

Then our body parts started flying in the air.

"Oh, sorry about that. . .I'd better use the other hand," Steve said.

We all looked over at what was left of Herobrine.

189

All that was left was a Herobrine skin suit lying on the ground.

Steve and I just looked at each other and smiled because we both had the same idea.

"Who needs a new Minecraft skin?" me and Steve asked everybody.

Then we all just burst out laughing.

Saturday

Well, yesterday all of Minecraft was almost destroyed. . .again.

Not to mention I almost lost the best friend I've ever had.

But I knew Steve could do it.

He just needed a little help from his pals.

Herobrine got what he deserved, though.

Now he can't bully anybody else ever again.

That's because Steve took all his bones and donated them to the local village farm for bone meal.

191

They used his bones to grow some really hot jalapeños. You know, for the spicy booger snacks.

As for Herobrine, Old Man Jenkins patched him up so now he just floats around moaning and groaning about how unfair life is.

But, he sure makes a great piñata at parties.

Especially at night.

The good news is that Rachel calmed down a little bit, too.

I think it had something to do with breaking the curse that was on her dad.

Yeah, after we turned the Witch into Witch juice, the curse was broken and her dad went back to only having one head now.

But I have to admit, it must be pretty sweet having two less parents around.

And Rachel even tried to, sorta, almost, maybe, apologize for traumatizing me these past few weeks. . .

"Hey, Zack," Rachel said.

"What is it now, Rachel?"

"I just wanted to say. . .um. . .stay outta trouble or the Ender-zombie is going to get you, OK?" she said.

"Thanks. . .I think."

"Oh, and here," she said, handing me a dusty book. "Don't leave this thing lying around or somebody might read all your embarrassing secrets. You never know what people might do with that kind of information."

"Uh. . .thanks?"

Then she walked away with a look on her face that either meant she was proud of me or that she planned to murder me in my sleep.

Oh, and about Carrie.

We kinda decided to just be friends.

I mean, don't get me wrong. Carrie is a cool girl.

Not to mention that having a high school girlfriend would probably make me a god in middle school.

You can't even buy that kind of street cred.

But, I kinda realized, I think have enough drama in my life right now without Carrie.

I mean, I like her passion. She's the kind of girl Dirk Craftly would totally go out with.

But, man! High school girls are intense!

Oh, and if you didn't know, I'm now the biggest Noob in the entire Minecraft overworld.

But you know, I really don't mind being a Noob anymore.

Because I finally realize that my real friends don't care if I'm a Noob, or a Zombie, or a basket case, or a jock, or a geek.

They just care that I'm me.

And I can live with that.

And since my Noob and Proud video went viral, Ellie asked me to do another one.

Except this time, not only did I sing the Noob and Proud song, but I showed off some of my sweet moves too.

Moves like this. . .

Mmph! Mmph! Mmph! Mmph!

Yeah!

Superstah!

THE END

Find out What Happens Next in...

Diary of a Minecraft Zombie Book 14
"Cloudy with a Chance of Apocalypse"

Get Your Copy on Amazon Today!

Please Leave Us a Review

Please support us by leaving a review.
The more reviews we get, the more
books we will write!

And if you really liked this book,
please tell a friend.

I'm sure they will be happy you told
them about it.

Check Out All of Our Books in the Diary of a Minecraft Zombie Series

The Diary of a Minecraft Zombie Book 1
"A Scare of a Dare"

In the first book of this hilarious Minecraft adventure series, take a peek in the diary of an actual 12 year old Minecraft Zombie and all the trouble he gets into in middle school.

Get Your Copy Today!

The Diary of a Minecraft Zombie Book 2
"Bullies and Buddies"

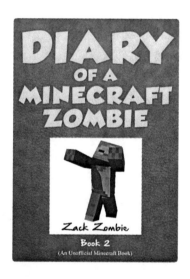

This time Zombie is up against some of the
meanest and scariest mob bullies at school.
Will he be able to stop the mob bullies from
terrorizing him and his friends, and make it
back in one piece?

Jump into the Adventure
and Find Out!

The Diary of a Minecraft Zombie Book 3
"When Nature Calls"

What does a Zombie do for Spring break?
Find out in this next installment of the exciting
and hilarious adventures of a Minecraft Zombie!

Get Your Copy Today!

The Diary of a Minecraft Zombie Book 4
"Zombie Swap"

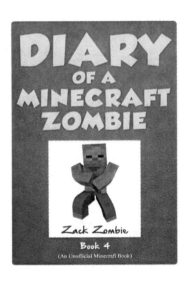

Zombie and Steve have Switched Bodies!

Find out what happens as Zombie
has to pretend to be human and Steve
pretends to be a zombie.

Jump into this Zany
Adventure Today!

The Diary of a Minecraft Zombie Book 5
"School Daze"

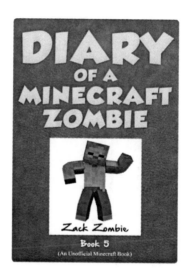

Summer Vacation is Almost Here and
Zombie Just Can't Wait!

Join Zombie on a Hilarious Adventure as
he tries to make it through the last few weeks
before Summer Break.

Jump into the
Adventure Today!

The Diary of a Minecraft Zombie Book 6
"Zombie Goes To Camp"

Join Zombie, as he faces his biggest fears,
and tries to survive the next 3 weeks at
Creepaway Camp.

Will he make it back in one piece?

Jump into His Crazy Summer Adventure and Find Out!

The Diary of a Minecraft Zombie Book 7
"Zombie Family Reunion"

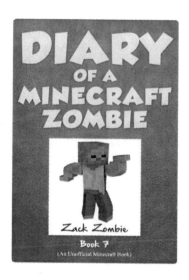

Join Zombie and his family on their crazy adventure as they face multiple challenges trying to get to their 100th Year Zombie Family Reunion.

Will Zombie even make it?

Get Your Copy Today and Find Out!

The Diary of a Minecraft Zombie Book 8
"Back to Scare School"

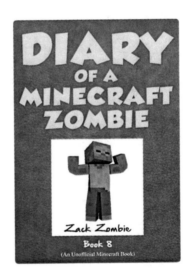

Zombie finally made it through 7th grade...
And he even made it through one really crazy
summer! But will Zombie be able to survive
through the first weeks of being an 8th grader
in Mob Scare School?

Find Out in His Latest Adventure Today!

The Diary of a Minecraft Zombie Book 9
"Zombie's Birthday Apocalypse"

It's Halloween and it's Zombie's Birthday! But there's a Zombie Apocalypse happening that may totally ruin his Birthday party. Will Zombie and his friends be able to stop the Zombie Apocalypse so that they can finally enjoy some cake and cookies at Zombie's Birthday Bash?

Jump into the Adventure and Find Out!

The Diary of a Minecraft Zombie Book 10
"One Bad Apple"

There's a new kid at Zombie's middle school and everyone thinks he is so cool. But the more Zombie hangs out with him, the more trouble he gets into. Is this new Mob kid as cool as everyone thinks he is, or is he really a Minecraft Wolf in Sheep's clothing?

Jump Into this Zany Minecraft Adventure and Find Out!

The Diary of a Minecraft Zombie Book 11
"Insides Out"

In his latest zany adventure, Zombie has to deal with one of the biggest challenges he's ever faced in his preteen life…His feelings.

Will Zombie be able to get a grip? Or will his pre-teen angst get the better of him?

Jump Into this Crazy Minecraft Adventure and Find Out!

The Diary of a Minecraft Zombie Book 12
"Pixelmon Gone"

Zombie Has Discovered New and Amazing
Creatures in the Minecraft World called Pixelmon!
Except little by little the Pixelmon are disappearing
and nobody knows why. Can Zombie, Steve and
their Minecraft friends save the Pixelmon from utter
extinction? Or will they get into even more wacky
trouble than ever before?

Jump Into Another of Zombie's Zany Minecraft Adventures and Find Out!

CPSIA information can be obtained
at www.ICGtesting.com
Printed in the USA
LVOW07s1729191017
553031LV00010B/336/P